Mummy Time

Judith Kerr

For my wonderful
sister-in-law,
Diana Kerr

First published in hardback in Great Britain
by HarperCollins Children's Books in 2018
First published in paperback in 2020

10 9 8 7 6 5 4 3 2 1

ISBN: 978-0-00-830683-0

HarperCollins Children's Books is a division of HarperCollins Publishers Ltd.

Text and illustrations copyright © Kerr-Kneale Productions Ltd 2018

Visit our website at www.harpercollins.co.uk

Printed and bound in China

MIX
Paper from
responsible sources
FSC™ C007454

This book is produced from independently certified FSC™ paper
to ensure responsible forest management.

For more information visit: www.harpercollins.co.uk/green

"…just taking the little one out
for a bit of mummy time…

… but my dear, the party last night…
some very odd faces there,
I thought…

…yes, the one with the awful teeth…

…actually he was rather sweet…

…but the food…
I know she had a lot
of mouths to feed…

…well, all I can say is, different
people have different tastes…

… I suppose they wanted to make
a bit of a splash. Before this they
could barely keep their heads
above water. But they saw this
chance and grabbed it with both hands…

…and now they're riding high…

…which is not how things are with us.
Luck just seems to pass us by these days…

*…and I'm sort of used
to just hanging on…*

…and living from hand to mouth…

…but then something happens…

…and you come down to earth with a bump…

…the other day in a shop I saw this beautiful little striped woolly which would have been perfect for me…

… but of course I couldn't have it …

… but I really loved it …

…and I just burst into tears. It was awful.

Everyone was looking at me…

… but, my dear, I'm sorry you've had
to listen to all this misery…

… I expect that sooner or later
something good will come our way again…

*…and as long as I've got the
little one, and a friend like yourself,
I can't complain…*

*…which reminds me
I'd better go and see
where he's got to."*

"Come on then. Say goodbye
to that smelly doggie, and
we'll go home for tea.

We had a nice time, didn't we?"